Top 10 QUARTERBACKS

Chris W. Sehnert

ABDO & Daughters
Publishing

Published by Abdo & Daughters, 4940 Viking Drive, Suite 622, Edina, Minnesota 55435.

Copyright © 1997 by Abdo Consulting Group, Inc., Pentagon Tower, P.O. Box 36036, Minneapolis, Minnesota 55435 USA. International copyrights reserved in all countries. No part of this book may be reproduced in any form without written permission from the publisher.

Printed in the United States.

Cover and Interior Photo credits: Allsports Photos
Wide World Photos
Bettmann Photos
Sports Illustrated

Edited by Paul Joseph

Library of Congress Cataloging-in-Publication Data

Sehnert, Chris W.
      Top 10 Quarterbacks/ by Chris W. Sehnert
            p   cm. -- (Top 10 Champions)
      Includes index.
      Summary: Covers the careers and statistics of ten NFL quarterbacks:Steve Young, Johnny Unitas, Bart Starr, Joe Namath, Roger Staubach, Bob Griese, Terry Bradshaw, Jim Plunkett, Joe Montana, and Troy Aikman.
      ISBN 1-56239-791-5
      1. Football players--United States--Biography--Juvenile literature. 2. Football players--rating of--United States--Juvenile literature 3. Quarterback (football)--Juvenile literature. [1. Football players.] I. Title. II. Series: Sehnert, Chris W. Top 10 Champions.
      GV939.A1S37   1997
      796.332'092'2--dc21   96-52410
      [B]   CIP
                                                      AC

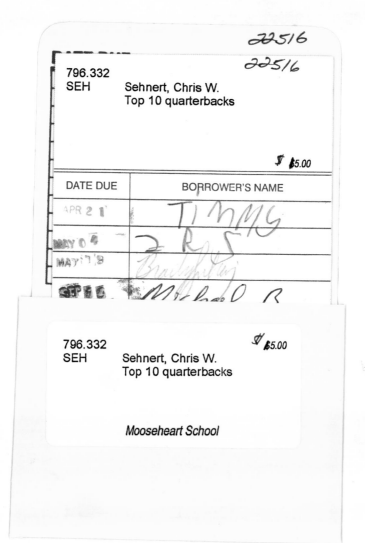

22516

22516

796.332
SEH   Sehnert, Chris W.
           Top 10 quarterbacks

$5.00

DATE DUE	BORROWER'S NAME
APR 2 1	TIMMS
MAY 0 4	2 R S
MAY 1 9	Bradley Riley
SEP 1 6	Michael R

Table of Contents

Johnny UNITAS

When people rise above all odds to become champions, they are embraced by their followers as true heroes. Johnny Unitas was this type of champion for the National Football League (NFL). Unitas was the strong-armed quarterback of the Baltimore Colts from 1956-1972. He led the team to three NFL Championships on his way to becoming one of the greatest passers the game of football has ever known. Unitas was heralded as a "working-class hero," not only for his hard-nosed style of play, but for the difficult path he followed to greatness.

John Unitas grew up in Pittsburgh, Pennsylvania. He was the third of four children born to Helen and Leonard Unitas. When Johnny was five years old, his father died. Helen went to work to support the family. Her example of courage and persistence was a great inspiration to Johnny. He later credited her for teaching him what it takes to be a winner.

Johnny attended St. Justin's High School, and played quarterback for the football team. Because of his family's hardships, he would need a scholarship to go on to college. Johnny's great skills were known to many college scouts, but his slender, 145-pound body kept scholarship offers away. When the University of Louisville in Kentucky came with an offer, Johnny eagerly accepted, despite the small size of Louisville's football program. In his four seasons as a Louisville Cardinal, Johnny set a school record with 27 touchdown (TD) passes. He also put on the additional weight he would need to join the NFL.

The Pittsburgh Steelers drafted Johnny in 1955. He did not make the team. Johnny took a job working construction, and played football in a Pittsburgh city league for $6 per game. The next season, he was signed by the Baltimore Colts as a backup to their starting quarterback (QB) George Shaw. When Shaw was injured during the fourth game of the 1956 season, Johnny finally got his chance. His first pass was intercepted and returned for a TD. On three other possessions, he fumbled the ball. The Chicago Bears destroyed the Colts that day, 58-27. They did not destroy Johnny's confidence, however. Two weeks later, he led Baltimore to a 56-21 victory over the Los Angeles Rams!

In the following years Johnny Unitas became the most feared offensive weapon in all of professional football. He passed for more TDs (290) than any other quarterback who had come before him. He led the NFL in TD passes four seasons in a row (1957-1960), and passed for paydirt in a record 47-consecutive games. The Baltimore Colts won NFL Championships in 1958 and 1959. In 1960 and 1961, Johnny was named the Most

Valuable Player (MVP) in the NFL's annual Pro Bowl. The Colts lost to the Cleveland Browns in the 1964 NFL Championship, and were defeated by the New York Jets in Super Bowl III (1968).

In Super Bowl V (1970), Johnny Unitas returned to the league's championship for the final time. He threw the game's only TD pass, as the Baltimore Colts defeated the Dallas Cowboys. Johnny's great career was nearly over. He was traded to the San Diego Chargers in 1973 and retired the next year. A "working-class hero" who became a great champion, Johnny Unitas was inducted into the Pro Football Hall of Fame in 1979.

PROFILE
John Unitas
Born: May 7, 1933
Height: 6' 1"
Weight: 195 pounds
College: University of Louisville
Position: Quarterback
Teams: Baltimore Colts (1956-1972), San Diego Chargers (1973)

Championship

SEASONS

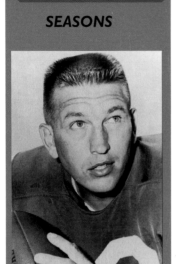

Johnny Unitas

1958
NFL Championship
Baltimore Colts (23) vs.
New York Giants (17)

1959
NFL Championship
Baltimore Colts (31) vs.
New York Giants (16)

1970-71
Super Bowl V
Baltimore Colts (16) vs.
Dallas Cowboys (13)

NFL
Record Book

Most Seasons Leading the League in Passing Attempts:
4- John Unitas (1957, 1959-1961)
4- Sammy Baugh (1937, 1943, 1947, 1948)
4- George Blanda (1953, 1963-1965)
4- Dan Marino (1984, 1986, 1988, 1992)

Most Consecutive Seasons Leading the League in
Passing Attempts:
3- John Unitas (1959-1961)
3- George Blanda (1963-1965)

Most Seasons Leading the League in Touchdowns:
4- John Unitas (1957-1960)
4- Len Dawson (1962-1963, 1965-1966)

Most Consecutive Games with a Touchdown Pass:
47- John Unitas (1956-1960)
30- Dan Marino (1985-1987)

Most Touchdown Passes, Career:
352- Dan Marino (1983-)
342- Fran Tarkenton (1961-1978)
290- John Unitas (1956-1973)

Longest Pass Completions, Super Bowl:
80 yds- Jim Plunkett, 1981 Oakland vs. Philadelphia
80 yds- Doug Williams, 1988 Washington vs. Denver
76 yds- David Woodley, 1983 Miami vs. Washington
75 yds- John Unitas, 1971 Baltimore vs. Dallas
75 yds- Terry Bradshaw, 1979 Pittsburgh vs. Dallas

OUTSIDE THE LINES

Johnny married his high school sweetheart, Dorothy Jean Hoelle. They have six children.

Johnny's "Flat-Top" haircut added to his reputation as a "Working-Class Hero."

Johnny Unitas (19) follows a blocker into the endzone.

AWARDS

1950- Selected as quarterback for Pittsburgh's All Catholic High School Team

1957- Jim Thorpe Trophy, for NFL's Most Valuable Player (MVP)

1959- Bert Bell Memorial Award, for NFL's most outstanding player

1960- MVP NFL Pro Bowl

1961- MVP NFL Pro Bowl

1967- Player of the Year, "Sporting News"

1979- Inducted into Pro Football Hall of Fame

Johnny Unitas far right

Bart
STARR

Vince Lombardi coached the Green Bay Packers to five World Championships in his nine seasons with the team (1959-1967). His philosophy of coaching centered around the belief that "The team which errs the least wins the most." Lombardi was also a master of building confidence and character in his players through what he called "mental toughness." Among the toughest of Lombardi's many students was Green Bay's quarterback (QB), Bart Starr. Following the coach's theory, Bart kept his mistakes to a minimum. In the process, Starr became one of the NFL's all-time greatest champions!

Bryan Bartlett Starr was born and raised on a military air base in Montgomery, Alabama. His father, Ben Starr, was a United States Army Air Corps master sergeant. Bart's younger brother, Hilton, died from a tetanus infection at the age of 10. "We had a lot of fun growing up together," Bart recalls. "I think he would have been the better athlete of the two of us."

When Bart was 12 years old, he began playing football for a YMCA team in Birmingham, Alabama. At Sidney Lanier High School in Montgomery, Bart was a backup QB until his junior season. In his senior year, he was chosen to play in the high school All-American game in Memphis, Tennessee.

Bart entered the University of Alabama in 1952, where he became the starting QB for the Crimson Tide as a college freshman. He led the team to a 61-6 blowout victory over Syracuse in the Orange Bowl on New Year's Day, 1953.

The following season, he took Alabama to the Cotton Bowl. Bart injured his back during his junior season and returned to the bench as a college senior. J. B. Whitworth became Alabama's new coach that season and decided to start with a younger lineup. The decision was a major disappointment to Bart. Three years later, Whitworth would be replaced by the legendary Bear Bryant, while Bart was on his way to professional football immortality.

The Green Bay Packers selected Bart in the 17th-round of the 1956 NFL draft. He had begun to lose confidence in his own abilities, but he tried hard to make the team. "I didn't know I had made it until the last cut," Bart said. "When I stuck, it was one of the happiest moments of my life." He spent his first three seasons as Green Bay's second-string QB.

The Packers won only one game in 1958. The next season, Vince Lombardi became their new coach. When Green Bay's starting QB was injured during the 1959 season, Bart was given an opportunity to play. One of his early mistakes angered Lombardi, and the coach shouted "Starr! You could see that ball was going to be intercepted when you threw it. One more like

that and you're gone!" The lesson of mental toughness was beginning to set-in. Bart told his wife, Cherry, "If, when I throw a ball that's intercepted, I say to myself, 'What's the use?' I think that everything I throw is going to be intercepted. Instead, I have to tell myself that the next pass I throw will be for a touchdown."

Over the next 12 seasons, Bart became one of the most accurate passers in NFL history. He set a record for consecutive passes without an interception (294), and led the NFL in passing three times. Bart was an important part in all five of the Packers' championship seasons. After their 1966 NFL title, Green Bay defeated the Champions of the American Football League (AFL) in what would later become known as Super Bowl I. The Packers returned the next year to win Super Bowl II. Bart Starr's playing career ended after the 1971 season. He was inducted into the Pro Football Hall of Fame in 1977.

PROFILE
Bart Starr
Born: January 9, 1934
Height: 6' 1"
Weight: 200 pounds
College: University of Alabama
Position: Quarterback
Teams: Green Bay Packers (1956-1971)

PORTRAIT OF A CHAMPION

CHAMPIONSHIP
SEASONS

Bart Starr hands off.

1961
NFL Championship
Green Bay Packers (37) vs. New York Giants (0)

1962
NFL Championship
Green Bay Packers (16) vs. New York Giants (7)

1965
NFL Championship
Green Bay Packers (23) vs. Cleveland Browns (12)

1966-67
Super Bowl I
Green Bay Packers (35) vs. Kansas City Chiefs (10)

1967-68
Super Bowl II
Green Bay Packers (33) vs. Oakland Raiders (14)

AWARDS AND HONORS

1951- Selected as Quarterback for the High School All-American game

1962- NFL's Leading Passer: 285-Attempts/ 178-Completions/ 2438-yards/ 12-TD/ 9-Int.

1964- NFL's Leading Passer: 272-Attempts/ 163-Completions/ 2144-Yards/ 15-TD/ 4-Int.

1965- Named Wisconsin Athlete of the Year

1966- NFL's Leading Passer: 251-Attempts/ 156-Completions/ 2257-Yards/ 14-TD/ 3-Int.

1966- Jim Thorpe Trophy, for NFL's Most Valuable Player (MVP)

1967- Super Bowl MVP

1968- Super Bowl MVP

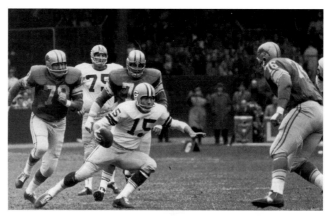

Bart Starr scrambling to make a pass.

ICE BOWL

The 1967 NFL Championship game was played in frigid conditions (-15° F.) at Green Bay's Lambeau Field. Bart scored a touchdown on a QB sneak in the closing seconds of the game, to defeat the Dallas Cowboys. The victory sent the Packers to their second straight Super Bowl.

Bart Starr crossing the goal line during the Ice Bowl.

SIDELINES

Bart became the head coach of the Green Bay Packers in 1975. He was unable to lead the team back to the playoffs, during his nine year tenure (1975-1983) on the sidelines.

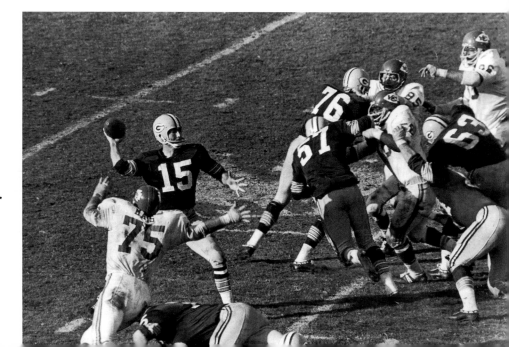

Bart Starr sets up to pass.

Joe NAMATH

To guarantee a victory in the National Football League (NFL) is not something most players would be willing to try. To deliver on that guarantee, when your team is an 18-point underdog, is even more astounding. As baseball legend Dizzy Dean once said, "It ain't braggin' if you can do it!" When the New York Jets defeated the Baltimore Colts in Super Bowl III (1968), Joe Namath had delivered on his word. The Jets were World Champions. "Broadway Joe" had guaranteed it!

Joseph William Namath was the youngest of five children. His parents were divorced when he was 12 years old. Both were later remarried. Joe's father was born in Hungary and immigrated to the United States at the age of 12. He worked in the steel mills of Beaver Falls, Pennsylvania, where Joe was raised.

Joe learned to throw a football at an early age. His older brothers regularly employed little "Joe Willie" as quarterback (QB) in their front yard games, promising never to tackle him. "Joe got so he could throw the ball out of sight, and he could hit a stump 40 yards away," his mother claims. At Beaver Falls High School, Joe starred in football, baseball, and basketball. Before graduating, 52 colleges and universities invited him to apply. He was also courted by six Major League Baseball teams.

The University of Alabama gave Joe a four-year scholarship and he became their starting QB in his sophomore season. The head coach of the Crimson Tide was the legendary Paul "Bear" Bryant. College football's all-time winningest coach showed no favoritism toward his star QB. When Joe broke curfew late in his junior season, he was suspended by Bryant, and forced to miss the Sugar Bowl. Bear would later say, "Joe was the greatest athlete I ever coached."

While Joe was playing his senior season at Alabama (1964), the American Football League (AFL) was completing its fifth season. The renegade circuit had only begun to challenge the more established NFL as professional football's dominant league. When Joe Namath signed with the AFL's New York Jets in 1965, the new league had its first star attraction. "Broadway Joe" was the AFL Rookie of the Year that season. Super Bowl I was played after the next season, matching the champions from both leagues.

Joe led the Jets to the AFL Championship in 1968. The Baltimore Colts won the NFL Championship that season and were expected to trounce the Jets in the Super Bowl. Four days before Super Sunday, Joe guaranteed a New York victory.

When the Jets upset the Colts in Super Bowl III, they became the first AFL team to win a World Championship. Two years later, the leagues merged.

Joe Namath played 12 seasons for the New York Jets (1965-1976). He finished his career with the Los Angeles Rams in 1977. While he never returned to the Super Bowl, his legendary status was secure. "Broadway Joe" was inducted into the Professional Football Hall of Fame in 1985.

PROFILE:
Joe Namath
Born: May 31, 1943
Height: 6' 2"
Weight: 195 pounds
College: University of Alabama
Position: Quarterback
Teams: New York Jets (1965-1976),
        Los Angeles Rams (1977)

PORTRAIT OF A CHAMPION

CHAMPIONSHIP
SEASONS

Joe Namath talking with his coach.

1968-69
Super Bowl III
New York Jets (16) vs. Baltimore Colts (7)

MILESTONES

1965- First Round Draft Pick, New York Jets

1965- AFL Rookie-of-the-Year

1966- Most Passing Yardage AFL (3,379)

1966- Most Valuable Player (MVP) AFL All-Star Game

1967- Most Passing Yardage AFL (4,007)

1967- First QB in Professional Football history to pass for 4,000 yards in a season

1968- AFL MVP

1969- Super Bowl MVP

1972- Most Passing Yardage AFC (2,816)

Joe Namath passing for his college, Alabama.

OUTSIDE THE LINES

Joe was considered professional football's most eligible bachelor during his playing days.

Joe displayed confidence on and off the football field. He once said, "I can't wait until tomorrow, 'cause I get better looking each day!"

Broadway Joe's popularity brought him many product endorsements. In his most memorable commercial, Joe appeared in panty-hose!

Joe Namath with the Jets.

Joe's other interests include golf and bowling.

PLAYING WITH PAIN

Joe injured his right knee while playing for the University of Alabama. Throughout his professional career, he required frequent surgeries on both knees. He made up for his lack of mobility with a strong throwing arm and a quick release of the football.

Joe Namath handing off.

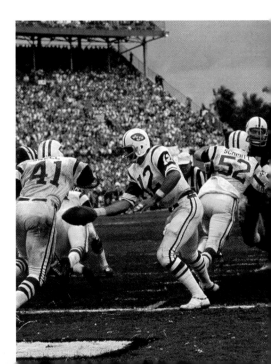

Roger
STAUBACH

The Dallas Cowboys began their NFL history as a struggling expansion team in 1960. By the end of their first decade, Dallas had made four straight playoff appearances, but were without an NFL Championship. After the 1970 season, Roger Staubach watched from the sidelines as his Cowboys were defeated by the Baltimore Colts in Super Bowl V. The next season, Roger took over the starting QB position, and led Dallas to their second straight NFC Title. With Roger in command, the Cowboys captured their first World Championship by defeating the Miami Dolphins in Super Bowl VI. The Dallas Cowboys had become known as "America's Team," and Roger Staubach was "Captain America!"

Roger Thomas Staubach was the only child of Robert and Betty Staubach. He was born and raised in Cincinnati, Ohio. Roger's mother wanted her son to study music, but by the age of seven, he was already developing a passion for sports. Baseball, basketball, and football were his favorite activities, and he was also an above-average student. In high school, Roger was selected by Cincinnati's All-City basketball team and was a star attraction on the football field. As a senior, he was elected president of Purcell High School's graduating class.

Several colleges and universities offered Roger athletic scholarships for football or basketball. He chose to play football for the United States Naval Academy at Annapolis, Maryland. In the 1963 season, Roger helped catapult Navy to a 9-1 record with his adept passing and scrambling style. Navy finished second in college football's national rankings that season, after a loss to top-ranked Texas in the Cotton Bowl. Roger was awarded the Heisman Trophy as the most outstanding collegiate football player in the United States.

The Cowboys signed Roger to a contract in 1965, but he delayed his professional football career to serve in the United States Navy. He became a veteran of the Vietnam War before joining Dallas for the 1969 season. His experience aboard rolling warships was a unique preparation for the NFL.

In Roger's third season with the Cowboys, he began to alternate with Craig Morton in the starting-QB position. By mid-season, the job belonged to only Roger. Commanding the helm, he steered Dallas to a 10-game winning streak culminated by their victory in Super Bowl VI. Roger received the Most Valuable Player Award (MVP) for the game. His Hall-of-Fame career had only begun.

Over the next eight seasons, Roger guided the Cowboys to the Super Bowl three more times. Dallas defeated the Denver Broncos in Super Bowl XII to become World Champions for the second time. Before retiring after the 1979 season, Roger became one of the highest ranked passers in the history of professional football. From College All-American to Captain of "America's Team," Roger Staubach was both an American hero and a true champion.

PROFILE:
Roger Staubach
Born: February 5, 1942
Height: 6' 3"
Weight: 202 pounds
College: United States Naval Academy
Position: Quarterback
Teams: Dallas Cowboys (1969-1979)

CHAMPIONSHIP
SEASONS

Roger Staubach lets go a pass while playing with the Dallas Cowboys.

1971-72
Super Bowl VI
Dallas Cowboys (24) vs. Miami Dolphins (3)

1977-78
Super Bowl XII
Dallas Cowboys (27) vs. Denver Broncos (10)

HAIL MARY!

Roger was an altar boy in the Catholic Church while growing up in Cincinnati. His devout faith carried over to his professional football career. With time running out in a 1975 playoff game, Roger completed a 50-yard TD pass to Drew Pearson. The Cowboys defeated the Minnesota Vikings (17-14) and later advanced to Super Bowl X. When asked to describe the miraculous game-winning play, Roger admitted never seeing Pearson catch the ball. "It was just a prayer," he said, "a Hail Mary!"

Staubach throwing on the run while quarterbacking for Navy.

Awards and HONORS

1960- Cincinnati All-City High School Basketball Team

1962- Thompson Trophy, Naval Academy's annual athletic award

1963- Thompson Trophy, Navy Academy's annual athletic award

1963- Heisman Trophy, Most outstanding intercollegiate football player

1964- Thompson Trophy, Naval Academy's annual athletic award

1965- Sword Award, Naval Academy Athletic Association for overall athletic contribution

1971- Highest Rated Passer- NFC (National Football Conference)

1971- NFL MVP

1972- Super Bowl MVP

1973- Highest Rated Passer- NFC

1977- Highest Rated Passer- NFC

1978- Highest Rated Passer- NFC

1979- Highest Rated Passer- NFC

1985- Inducted into Pro Football Hall of Fame

Roger Staubach after winning the Heisman Trophy.

FAST FACTS

-Roger also starred for Navy's Varsity Baseball team in college.

-Roger is the Dallas Cowboy's All-Time leading passer (22,700-yards).

-Roger's uniform number (12) was retired by Navy and later by the Cowboys.

-Roger's blue eyes are colorblind.

Bob
GRIESE

Football is a game of giant men. It is a battle of strength, where winning requires grit, guts, and determination. It is also a game of strategy, where calling the correct play is often as important as making the big hit. Bob Griese called the plays for the Miami Dolphins for 14 seasons. As football players go, Bob was a small and quiet man. He used his intelligence and ability in guiding Miami to a pair of Super Bowl Championships in the 1970s.

Bob Griese was born in Evansville, Indiana. He has an older brother and a younger sister. Their father died when Bob was 10 years old. Bob's mother raised her three children on the wages she earned as a secretary. Without a father, Bob relied on his coaches for much of his early upbringing. "A father is really a coach," he later would say. "And coaches became a kind of substitute father for me."

Bob paid close attention to what his coaches taught him, and it soon paid off. At Rex Mundi High School in Evansville, he was quarterback of the football team, and was already showing his talent for making decisions. One of his high school coaches called Bob "a kind of player-coach" for the way he often gave advice. He drew the attention of colleges and universities around the nation.

Notre Dame University was Bob's first choice of colleges to attend. Unfortunately, it was also one of the few major universities not to offer him a scholarship. Determined to remain in Indiana, he chose Purdue University. In his junior season, Bob's Purdue Boilermakers faced the top-ranked Fighting Irish of Notre Dame. Bob completed 19 of his 22 passes that day to upset the team that had spurned him two years earlier. The following season, Bob was selected as an All-American, and led Purdue to their first ever Rose Bowl victory!

The Miami Dolphins selected Bob in the first round of the 1967 NFL Draft. He was forced into action early in his rookie season when starting QB John Stofa suffered a broken ankle in the first regular season game. Later that season, he set an NFL record for throwing 122 passes without an interception. He was already being touted as a wise leader and an excellent offensive strategist.

Don Shula became the Dolphins' head coach in 1970. He was immediately impressed with Bob's ability to read defenses. "Bob will study the defenses against the run as hard as he will study the defenses against the pass. That's highly unusual for a quarterback," Shula said. This emphasis on the running game soon became a trademark for Miami's great teams of the 1970s. With Larry Csonka and Jim Kiick pounding the ball inside, and Mercury Morris speeding around the ends, opposing defenses had little choice but to protect against the ground game. Then without warning, Bob would fire the ball downfield to Paul Warfield, and the Dolphins would put six more points on the scoreboard.

Miami was defeated by the Dallas Cowboys in Super Bowl VI (January, 1972). The next season, the Dolphins returned to become the only team in NFL history to play an entire season without a loss (17-0). They followed their perfect season with a second straight NFL Championship, in Super Bowl VIII. Bob Griese retired after the 1980 season. He was inducted into the Pro Football Hall of Fame 10 years later.

PROFILE:
Bob Griese
Born: February 3, 1945
Height: 6' 1"
Weight: 190 pounds
Position: Quarterback
College: Purdue University
Teams: Miami Dolphins (1967-1980)

CHAMPIONSHIP
SEASONS

Bob Griese scrambles for the Dolphins.

1972-73
Super Bowl VII
Miami Dolphins (14) vs. Washington Redskins (7)

1973-74
Super Bowl VIII
Miami Dolphins (24) vs. Minnesota Vikings (7)

QUIET LEADER

Bob Griese's personality has been described as quiet and conservative. "I think I am more of an introvert than an extrovert," Bob admits, "I'm not loud or outspoken. And I'd still just as soon be off by myself as be with a group. But if there are a bunch of football players ready to play football, somebody has to be in command. Taking command of the situation, that's something that somehow I have always been able to do."

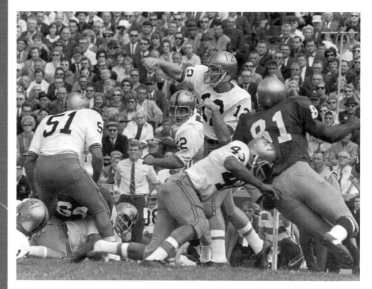

Bob Griese fires a pass for Purdue University.

17-0

Bob suffered a broken ankle in the fifth game of Miami's perfect 1972 season. He was forced to watch from the sidelines, while veteran Earl Morral led the Dolphins. Morral completed the regular-season, and helped Miami to victory in the first round of the AFC playoffs. In the AFC Championship game, however, the Dolphins were trailing the Pittsburgh Steelers 10-7 in the second half when Don Shula called on Bob to enter the game. With his ankle taped and tender, Bob engineered two TD drives and carried the Dolphins to their 16th-straight victory. Bob started Super Bowl VII, completed his first six passes, and capped-off a 17-0 season with Miami's victory over the Washington Redskins!

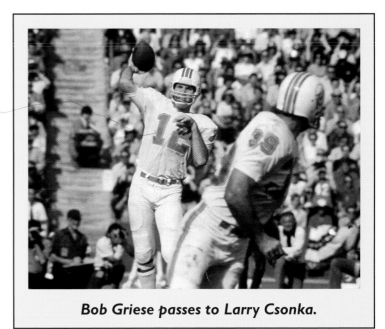

Bob Griese passes to Larry Csonka.

PASS THE TORCH

Bob's 14-year NFL career came to an end in 1980. Three years later the Dolphins drafted Dan Marino in the first-round. Marino has gone on to surpass Bob Griese as the Dolphins' all-time leading QB, and is the NFL's career leader in TD passes (352), Passing Yardage (48,841), and Pass Completions (3,913) through the 1995 season. Marino has yet to lead the Dolphins back to an NFL Championship, however.

Terry
BRADSHAW

The Pittsburgh Steelers became members of the NFL in 1933. Their beloved owner, Art Rooney, waited through 41 seasons without seeing his team win a championship. Suddenly in the 1970s, the Steelers' fortunes began to change. It began with a winning coin flip, which allowed Pittsburgh to make the first selection in the 1970 NFL Draft. With that pick, they chose Terry Bradshaw. In the years that followed, the Steelers surrounded their star QB with an abundance of talent. By the end of

the decade, the Pittsburgh Steelers had won more Super Bowl Championships than any team before them!

Terry Bradshaw grew up in a highly religious Southern Baptist family. His upbringing included regular Bible study and strict household rules. Terry's mother, Novis Bradshaw, took her three sons to revival meetings, where Terry often considered becoming a minister. After moving from Louisiana to Camanche, Iowa, Terry discovered professional football. His childhood hero was the Green Bay Packers' QB Bart Starr. Three years after moving to Iowa, the Bradshaws returned to Shreveport, Louisiana where Terry became QB on the Woodlawn High School football team.

Terry's biggest athletic accomplishment in high school did not take place in a football game. He set an American high school record throwing a javelin (244-feet, 11-inches). Several colleges and universities recruited Terry for track, but he accepted a football scholarship from Louisiana Tech. In his junior season, Terry led the team to the Gulf States Conference Championship. Louisiana Tech's victory in the Grantland Rice Bowl that season ranked them as the best small-college team in the country. After his senior season, Terry passed for 267 yards and 2 TDs in the College Senior Bowl. He earned the Most Valuable Player Award for the game.

The Pittsburgh Steelers and Chicago Bears finished the 1969 season in a tie with the NFL's worst records (1-13). Both teams wanted to make Terry their first-round draft choice. When the Bears called "heads" and the coin flip landed tails, the Steelers opened a new chapter in their storied history. Pittsburgh soon built a powerhouse lineup that included six future Hall of Famers.

Terry's transition to the professional ranks was not immediately successful. He struggled through two losing seasons, and was hampered by nagging injuries in a third. By the beginning of the 1974 season, he had lost the starting QB job to the popular "Jefferson Street Joe"

Gilliam. At mid-season, Terry returned to the starting lineup with renewed confidence. "It was as if he had hit rock bottom right before our eyes and pulled himself back up without anybody having to give him a hand," defensive tackle "Mean Joe" Greene observed. The Pittsburgh Steelers completed the season by defeating the Minnesota Vikings in Super Bowl IX.

With one World Championship behind him and his job securely in hand, Terry's Hall-of-Fame career began to blossom. Pittsburgh followed their first World Championship in 41 years by winning their second straight in Super Bowl X. Gradually, the Steelers' big-play offense became as well renowned as their devastating "Steel Curtain" defense. Terry's leadership earned him MVP honors in Super Bowl XIII, and again in Super Bowl XIV. He retired after the 1983 season.

PROFILE:

Terry Bradshaw
Born: September 2, 1948
Height: 6' 3"
Weight: 210 pounds
Position: Quarterback
College: Louisiana Tech
Teams: Pittsburgh Steelers (1970-1983)

CHAMPIONSHIP
SEASONS

1974-75
Super Bowl IX
Pittsburgh Steelers (16)
vs. Minnesota Vikings (6)

1975-76
Super Bowl X
Pittsburgh Steelers (21)
vs. Dallas Cowboys (17)

1978-79
Super Bowl XIII
Pittsburgh Steelers (35)
vs. Dallas Cowboys (31)

1979-80
Super Bowl XIV
Pittsburgh Steelers (31)
vs. Los Angeles Rams (19)

COIN TOSS

Art Rooney tried for a long time to bring an NFL Championship to Pittsburgh. By winning a simple coin-toss, he acquired a golden-haired QB with an arm to match. Terry Bradshaw led the Steelers to four Super Bowl titles on his way to becoming one of the greatest champions in NFL history. The long wait was over.

COUNTRY BUMPKIN

Terry's slow southern drawl and early struggles in the NFL led to a reputation as a dumb country-boy. In fact, he was one of the few QBs of his day to call his own plays in the huddle. He later reestablished his "country bumpkin" persona recording albums as a country and gospel singer.

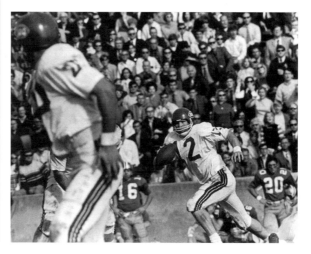

Bradshaw quarterbacking for Louisiana Tech.

STEELER Hall-of-Famers

Terry Bradshaw, inducted 1989

Arthur J. Rooney, inducted 1964, founder, Pittsburgh Steelers (1933-1982)

Chuck Noll, inducted 1993, coach, Pittsburgh Steelers (1969-1991)

Mel Blount, inducted 1989, cornerback, Pittsburgh Steelers (1970-1983)

Joe Greene, inducted 1987, defensive tackle, Pittsburgh Steelers (1969-1981)

Jack Ham, inducted 1988, linebacker, Pittsburgh Steelers (1971-1982)

Franco Harris, inducted 1990, running back, Pittsburgh Steelers (1972-1983)

Jack Lambert, inducted 1990, linebacker, Pittsburgh Steelers (1974-1984)

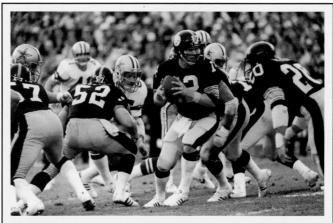

Bradshaw quarterbacking the Steelers.

WHO'S IN THE HALL?

Terry was inducted into the Professional Football Hall-of-Fame in 1989. Four of his five teammates, who are also members, belonged to the infamous "Steel Curtain" defense. The other is running back Franco Harris. Their coach Chuck Noll is also a Hall-of-Famer. As is the Steelers founder Art Rooney. John Stallworth and Lynn Swann were Terry's favorite wide receiver targets. They are probable future enshrinees.

Bradshaw fading back to pass.

27

Jim
PLUNKETT

The Oakland Raiders play football with a simple philosophy: "Just Win, Baby!" Behind this creed, put forth by their long-time chief executive Al Davis, the Raiders have built an intimidating reputation. On defense, they take on the mean-spirit of their one-eyed pirate mascot, stopping their opponents with bone-crushing tackles. Offensively, the Raiders prefer to strike quickly. For this reason Al Davis could see potential in the veteran arm of Jim Plunkett. A former college All-American, Plunkett had been cut after eight NFL seasons. He became the Raiders' second-string QB in 1979. Jim Plunkett's professional football career was far from over. He would soon take over as starting quarterback and lead the Raiders to a pair of Super Bowl Championships.

James William Plunkett was the youngest of three children, and the only son of William and Carmen Plunkett. He was born in San Jose, California. Jim's parents were born in New Mexico and were of Mexican-American descent. Both were legally blind. While financially poor, the Plunketts raised their children to have simple, basic values of honesty, proper manners, and respect for older people. As a child, Jim worked odd-jobs to help out the family income. He was big for his age, and he soon developed an interest for athletics. His favorite sport was football, and he would often travel to nearby Stanford University to watch their games.

In high school, Jim began taking athletics very seriously. He gave up basketball and joined the wrestling team to build strength for football. He also ran track and was a star on the baseball diamond. By the age of 17, he could throw a football over 85 yards! As a senior at James Lick High School in San Jose, Jim was selected to play QB in California's North-South All-Star Game. He graduated in 1966 and was heavily recruited by colleges and universities nationwide. For Jim, the choice was simple. He elected to stay close to home, and accepted an athletic scholarship from Stanford.

Jim's elation over his acceptance to Stanford was nearly squashed when doctors discovered a tumor in his neck. Fortunately, the benign growth was successfully removed. The surgery, however, marked the beginning of a difficult two-year recuperation period. In 1968, Jim returned to the football field as Stanford's starting QB and before long he was shattering nearly every Pacific Conference record for passing. As a senior, he carried Stanford to a conference championship and earned a trip to the Rose Bowl. Jim was named the game's MVP and was also awarded the 1970 Heisman Trophy.

The New England Patriots selected Jim as the first player taken in the 1971 NFL Draft. He was not a

disappointment. Jim became the first NFL rookie QB to play every offensive down for his team. He was named the Rookie of the Year in the American Football Conference (AFC). The Patriots, however, continued to struggle, and their inability to protect the QB was taking a toll on Jim's career. In 1976, he requested a trade to the San Francisco 49ers, where for two more seasons he labored on a less-than-spectacular squad.

The Raiders signed Jim as a back-up QB for Ken Stabler in 1978. "The Snake" had led Oakland to their first Super Bowl Championship two years earlier. Jim took over the starter's position in 1980 and led the Raiders to a second NFL Championship in Super Bowl XV. Three years after that, Jim Plunkett and the Raiders were Super Bowl Champions once again.

PROFILE:
Jim Plunkett
Born: December 5, 1947
Height: 6' 2"
Weight: 215 pounds
Position: Quarterback
College: Stanford University
Teams: New England Patriots (1971-1975), San Francisco 49ers (1976-1977), Oakland/ Los Angeles Raiders (1978-86)

PORTRAIT OF A CHAMPION

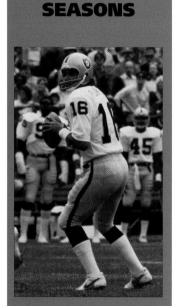

Jim Plunkett fades back to pass for the Raiders.

1980-81
Super Bowl XV
Oakland Raiders (27) vs. Philadelphia Eagles (10)

1983-84
Super Bowl XVIII
Los Angeles Raiders (38) vs. Washington Redskins (9)

GO DEEP

On October 2, 1983, Jim Plunkett connected with Cliff Branch for the longest pass completion in NFL history. After taking the snap at his own 1-yard line, Jim unloaded a bomb that Branch converted into a 99-yard TD reception. It is a feat that has been accomplished seven other times and can only be broken on a longer football field! Two years earlier Jim completed an 80-yard TD pass to Kenny King, which remains the longest pass completion in Super Bowl history.

Plunkett (16) quarterbacking for Standford University

RETURN TO SENDER

In 1982, the Raiders moved to Los Angeles, California. The switch came just two seasons after the team had won their second NFL Championship in Oakland. Amidst protests and lawsuits, renegade owner Al Davis eventually got what he wanted. The next season Jim Plunkett and the Raiders brought the city of Los Angeles their first Super Bowl Championship. The Raiders returned to Oakland in 1995.

STAY IN SCHOOL

Jim was tempted to leave Stanford University for the NFL after his junior season (1969). The death of his father earlier that year had left Jim's mother in need of financial help. He decided to stay in school out of loyalty to the Mexican-American children he was counseling at the time. "How could I tell them not to drop out of high school, if it looked like I was dropping out of Stanford," he said later.

Plunkett lets go a pass for the Raiders.

In the end, his decision worked out well. Jim's senior season at Stanford included a Pacific Conference Championship, a Rose Bowl victory over Ohio State, MVP Awards in both the Rose Bowl and the Hula Bowl (a college all-star game), a Heisman Trophy, and the No. 1 selection in the NFL Draft. He used his signing bonus to buy a house for his disabled mother.

Plunkett with the Heisman Trophy.

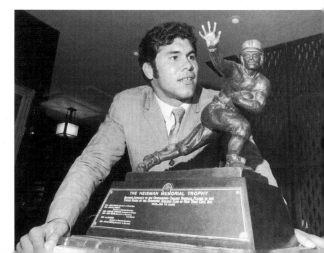

Joe MONTANA

In 1849, thousands of men and women rushed to the state of California seeking a fortune in gold. One hundred years later, the professional football team, named in memory of those exploits, lost in the championship game of the All-American Football Conference (AAFC). The next year (1950), the San Francisco 49ers joined the NFL where they played three decades without reaching another league championship game. In the 1980s the 49ers found their gold mine in Montana—not in the "Big Sky" state, but in a QB who was a master of executing the big play. Joe Montana led the San Francisco 49ers to four Super Bowl Championships in nine years. His exploits on the football gridiron became nearly as legendary as the mining 49ers themselves!

Joseph C. Montana Jr. was born in Monongahela, Pennsylvania. He was an only child. His father, Joe Sr., encouraged his son to develop his athletic skill at an early age. Little Joe received his first baseball and bat when he was eight months old. The Montana's backyard was soon converted into a playground, where Joe practiced for hours a day throwing footballs through swinging tires. His childhood hero was fellow Pennsylvanian, Joe Namath.

Montana was an all-around star athlete at Ringgold High School in Monongahela. Upon graduation, he nearly accepted a grant-in-aid to play basketball for North Carolina State University. He was then offered a scholarship to play football at the University of Notre Dame. Joe chose to play football. In his freshman season with the Notre Dame Fighting Irish, Joe gained a reputation as "the Comeback Kid." He was a third-string QB who twice came off the bench and led his team to last-minute victories. After sitting out his sophomore season with an injured shoulder, Joe returned to the bench in 1977. In the season's third game, the Irish were losing 24-10 to the Purdue Boilermakers. With the first-string QB out of sync, and the second-stringer out with an injury, Joe was summoned again to revive the Notre Dame offense. He passed for three TDs in the fourth quarter, as Notre Dame completed yet another miracle come-from-behind victory, 31-24. Joe took over the starting QB job from that day forward. He carried the Irish to a National Championship that season, with a victory over the Texas Longhorns in the Cotton Bowl.

Joe provided one more miracle in his final college performance. The Fighting Irish returned to the Cotton Bowl in January 1979. Joe became ill and sat out the first half on the bench. The Houston Cougars were leading Notre Dame

34-12 when the Comeback Kid took the field late in the third quarter. He completed the final pass of his college career as time ran out in the fourth quarter. When his receiver reached paydirt, Joe Montana had done it again, and Notre Dame had won its second straight Cotton Bowl, 35-34.

The San Francisco 49ers chose Joe in the third round of the 1979 NFL draft. After a season-and-a-half in a backup roll, he grabbed the reigns of the San Francisco offense late in the 1980 season. His first full-season as the starting QB ended with the 49ers victory in Super Bowl XVI. Joe was the game's MVP. It was an award he would win twice more on his way to leading San Francisco to three more NFL Championships.

PROFILE:
Joe Montana
Born: June 11, 1956
Height: 6' 2"
Weight: 195 pounds
Position: Quarterback
College: Notre Dame University
Teams: San Francisco 49ers (1979-1992), Kansas City Chiefs (1993-1994)

CHAMPIONSHIP

SEASONS

1981-82
Super Bowl XVI
San Francisco 49ers (26)
vs. Cincinnati Bengals (21)

1984-85
Super Bowl XIX
San Francisco 49ers (38)
vs. Miami Dolphins (16)

1988-89
Super Bowl XXIII
San Francisco 49ers (20)
vs. Cincinnati Bengals (16)

1989-90
Super Bowl XXIV
San Francisco 49ers (55)
vs. Denver Broncos (10)

THE CATCH

Joe's favorite receiver during the 49ers 1981 Super Bowl march was Dwight Clark. Joe and Dwight were San Francisco rookies together in 1979. Two years later, they connected for a TD in the NFC Championship game on a play known as "The Catch." The throw came out of desperation, as Joe was heavily pursued by the Dallas Cowboy defense. Dwight Clark leaped high in the air bringing the ball down in the back of the endzone with less than a minute remaining in the game. The play vaulted the San Francisco 49ers into their first NFL Championship game.

Joe Montana playing for the 49ers.

PITCHER PERFECT

Joe played in two Cotton Bowls and four Super Bowls. He led his team to victory each time. He was named the game's MVP in Super Bowl XVI, Super Bowl XIX, and Super Bowl XXIV. Joe's many Super Bowl records include Most Career TD Passes (11), Most Career Passing Yardage (1,142), Most Single Game Passing Yardage (357), Most Career Completions (83), and Highest Passer Rating (127.8). Perhaps his most amazing Super Bowl record is for Interception Percentage. Joe ranks second in Career Super Bowl Passing Attempts (122), and his Interception Percentage is a perfect 0%!

Joe Montana scrambles for Notre Dame University.

CHEMISTRY

Bill Walsh became the General Manager and Head Coach of the San Francisco 49ers in 1979. He chose Joe in the NFL Draft that season, hoping he could lead the team into the future. In the following seasons, Walsh drafted defensive back Ronnie Lott, running back Roger Craig, and wide receiver Jerry Rice. With Walsh's brilliance and the 49ers emphasis on organizational chemistry, San Francisco built a dynasty that became "The Team of the Eighties." Bill Walsh was inducted into the Pro Football Hall of Fame in 1993. He will soon have some familiar company.

Troy AIKMAN

America loves a winner. Winning year-in and year-out is how the Dallas Cowboys gained the reputation as "America's Team." In the 1980s, however, the Cowboys fell on hard times. In 1986, Dallas suffered through their first losing season (7-9) in over two decades. In 1988, they had the worst record (3-13) in professional football. It was time for a changing of the guard—and the QB as well. When millionaire oil man Jerry Jones purchased the Cowboys in 1989, a transformation was underway. Jones installed Jimmy Johnson to replace Tom Landry, who had been the only head coach in the Cowboys proud history. With the first pick in the 1989 NFL Draft, Jones and Johnson chose Troy Aikman. In a few short years, the Dallas Cowboys returned to familiar territory. America's Team was back on top.

Troy Kenneth Aikman was the youngest of Charlyn and Kenneth Aikman's three children. From the very beginning of his life, Troy was made to overcome adversity. He was born with deformed feet, which required him to wear corrective orthopedic shoes until he was three years old. At the age of 13, Troy's family moved from their home in Los Angeles, California, to a ranch in the small town of Henryetta, Oklahoma. At first, Troy was unhappy and unaccustomed to life on a farm. His family raised cattle, pigs, and chickens. Before long the teenaged Troy grew to appreciate small-town values. Troy was a star QB for the Henryetta High School football team. He was heavily recruited by the University of Oklahoma and

Oklahoma State University. Jimmy Johnson was Oklahoma State's head coach at the time, but Troy decided to play for Barry Switzer and the Oklahoma Sooners. Disappointed with Switzer's offense, which emphasized the running game, Troy transferred to the University of California at Los Angeles (UCLA) after his sophomore season. He became the Bruins starting QB in 1987, and led the team to a Cotton Bowl victory over Arkansas in his last college performance (January, 1989).

Jimmy Johnson had been watching Troy play football from the time he was a sophomore for the Henryetta Hens. With the first selection in the 1989 NFL Draft, Johnson made Troy a Cowboy. The transition to the pros, however, was not an easy one. Dallas won only one game in 1989—and that was a game in which Troy missed with an injury. Opposing defenses abused Troy with regularity. In one 1991 match-up, he was sacked 11 times by the Philadelphia Eagles. Jimmy Johnson would not give up on him. The next year Troy led the Cowboys all the way to victory in Super Bowl XXVII.

Troy had emerged as the NFL's top gun. The Dallas Cowboys were once again "America's Team." In 1993, Troy signed a $50-million contract, making him the highest paid player in NFL history. The Cowboys won the Super Bowl for the second straight time. Barry Switzer became the Cowboys' head coach in 1994 after Jimmy Johnson resigned over a dispute with Jerry Jones. In their first season under Troy's former college coach, the Cowboys were defeated by the San Francisco 49ers in the NFC Championship game. The next season, Troy and the Cowboys claimed their third Super Bowl Championship in four years!

PROFILE:
Troy Aikman
Born: November 21, 1966
Height: 6' 4"
Weight: 228 pounds
Position: Quarterback
Colleges: University of Oklahoma, UCLA (University of California at Los Angeles)
Team: Dallas Cowboys (1989-)

CHAMPIONSHIP
SEASONS

Troy Aikman triumphantly hoists the Super Bowl trophy.

1992-93
Super Bowl XXVII
Dallas Cowboys (52) vs. Buffalo Bills (17)

1993-94
Super Bowl XXVIII
Dallas Cowboys (30) vs. Buffalo Bills (13)

1995-96
Super Bowl XXX
Dallas Cowboys (27) vs. Pittsburgh Steelers (i7)

GOOD COMPANY

Troy shares the Cowboys backfield with one of the NFL's greatest running backs. Emmitt Smith has led the NFL in rushing four times since joining the Cowboys in 1990.

Troy along with Joe Montana (4) and Terry Bradshaw (4) are the only QBs to start and win at least three Super Bowls. None of the three players have ever lost an NFL Championship game!

Troy is closing-in on Roger Staubach (22,700 yards) as the Dallas Cowboys All-Time leading passer. He finished the 1995 season with 19,607 yards for his career.

Troy Aikman celebrates after completing a touchdown pass thrown in Super Bowl XXVII.

URBAN COWBOY

Troy's life has been split between living in one of the world's largest cities, and one of Oklahoma's smallest towns. He returned to his childhood home of Los Angeles, California, to complete his college career, but he refers to Henryetta, Oklahoma, as his hometown.

Troy now lives in the Dallas area where he enjoys working on his computer and socializing with family and friends. He is a fan of country music, and has appeared in a music video with the band Shenandoah. *People Magazine* voted him among its 50 Most Beautiful People. Troy claims to be shy, however, and he avoids the limelight while off the football field.

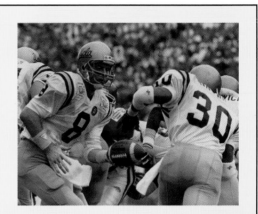

UCLA Quarterback Troy Aikman hands off to his running back.

Troy Aikman holds up his new jersey with NFL commissioner Pete Rozelle.

GIVING BACK

Troy is an active supporter of several charitable organizations. The Troy Aikman Foundation was established in 1991, and benefits children's charities in the Dallas-Fort Worth surrounding area. He also has taken part in Farm-Aid benefit concerts as part of the celebrity chorus.

YOUNG

One way to measure the greatness of champions is to examine their records. Another is by following their paths to greatness. Steve Young has been the NFL's leading passer for a record four straight times (1991-1994). He led the San Francisco 49ers to an NFL Championship in Super Bowl XXIX. He stands alone as the highest-rated quarterback in NFL history. Steve Young has followed a twisting, turning road to reach the very top of his profession.

Jon Steven Young was born in Salt Lake City, Utah. When he was eight years old, his family moved to Greenwich, Connecticut. Steve was the oldest of five children. He began playing football at nine years old. His boyhood hero was Roger Staubach. When Steve was a sophomore at Greenwich High School, his hands were hardly big enough to grip a football. He began to steadily improve himself as an athlete. As a high school senior he was captain of the football, basketball, and baseball teams! Steve returned to Utah in 1980, where he attended Brigham Young University (BYU). As a college freshman, he was regarded more for his running speed than his ability to throw. His coaches encouraged him to become a defensive back, but Steve was determined to make it as a QB. He worked hard to improve his arm strength and accuracy. The next season he became the Cougars' second-string passer behind Jim McMahon. Steve studied McMahon's leadership style from the sidelines week after week. McMahon finished his BYU career as one of the highest ranked QBs in college football history. He would go on to lead the Chicago Bears to victory in Super Bowl XX.

Meanwhile, Steve took over as the Cougars "Young Gun!"

In his two seasons as BYU's starting QB, Steve was heralded as one the most talented and versatile athletes in college football. He was an NCAA All-American in his senior season, and finished second in the Heisman Trophy balloting. Upon graduation, he was the most sought-after player in the 1984 NFL Draft. Steve, however, did not play in the NFL that season. Instead, he elected to sign a record-setting contract with the new USFL (United States Football League). Steve played two seasons with the Los Angeles Express before the renegade league crumbled under financial hardship. In 1985, he began his NFL career as a member of the Tampa Bay Buccaneers.

Steve's career in Tampa Bay also lasted two seasons. The Bucs were the worst team in professional football. They won four games and lost 28 times in 1985 and 1986. The offensive line was so poor at protecting the QB that one of Steve's coaches warned him to be careful. With 11 TD passes and 21 interceptions, Steve hardly seemed destined to become the NFL's

highest-rated passer. Nearly half of the passes he threw in those two seasons fell incomplete. In April 1987, he was traded to the San Francisco 49ers.

For the next four seasons, Steve served as a backup QB while Joe Montana led the 49ers to NFL Championships in Super Bowl XXIII and Super Bowl XXIV. When Montana was injured in the 1991 pre-season, Steve took over for the man many consider to be the greatest quarterback of all-time. Steve never relinquished the job. Under the close scrutiny of the San Francisco fans, he began his record string as the NFL's leading passer. He was the league's MVP in 1992, and guided the 49ers to their record-fifth NFL Championship two years later.

PROFILE:
Steve Young
Born: October 11, 1961
Height: 6' 2"
Weight: 200 pounds
Position: Quarterback
College: Brigham Young University
Teams: Los Angeles Express (1984-1985), Tampa Bay Buccaneers (1985-1986), San Francisco 49ers (1987-)

PORTRAIT OF A CHAMPION

CHAMPIONSHIP
SEASONS

![Steve Young with the 49ers.]

Steve Young with the 49ers.

1988-89
Super Bowl XXIII
San Francisco 49ers (20) vs.
Cincinnati Bengals (16)

1989-90
Super Bowl XXIV
San Francisco 49ers (55) vs.
Denver Broncos (10)

1994-95
Super Bowl XXIX
San Francisco 49ers (49) vs.
San Diego Chargers (26)

DOUBLE DUTY

The United States Football League (USFL) began play in 1983. Wealthy owners from the new league offered college stars huge sums of money in an attempt to rival the more established NFL. The USFL's season took place during the springtime rather than the traditional fall football season. Steve played two seasons with the new league. In 1985, he left the Los Angeles Express at the end of the USFL season, and joined the NFL's Tampa Bay Buccaneers that same fall.

LAWMAN

Steve was a star in the classroom as well as on the football field. While attending BYU, he completed a double-major in finance and international relations ahead of schedule. Because of his high marks, he was named one of the National Football Foundation and Hall of Fame's Scholar Athletes. He continued his education even after signing a multi-million dollar contract to play professional football. In 1993, Steve earned a post-graduate degree in law from BYU.

Steve Young quarterbacking for BYU.

GREAT-GREAT-GREAT

Brigham Young was Steve's great-great-great grandfather. He was the second president of the Mormon Church. In 1847, Brigham led his Mormon followers across the plains of the Midwestern United States to settle near the Great Salt Lake in Utah. He became Utah's first territorial governor and the namesake of Brigham Young University (BYU).

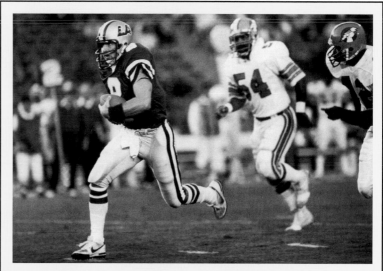

Steve Young playing for the LA Express.

Steve Young scrambles for the 49ers.

*R*ATINGS

The NFL's passer rating system combines QB statistics for TD passes, completions, yardage, and interceptions. In 1994, Steve's 112.8-rating surpassed Joe Montana's single season NFL record (112.4). Steve's career rating (96.1) currently ranks him as the highest rated passer in the history of the NFL!

Glossary

AFC: The American Football Conference. One of two conferences in the NFL.

All-American: A person chosen as the best amateur athlete at their position.

Contract: A written agreement a player signs when they are hired by a professional team.

Defense: The part of a team attempting to prevent the opposition from scoring.

Draft: A system in which new players are distributed to professional sports teams.

End-Zone: The area at either end of the playing field between the goal line and the end line that teams try to reach to score a touchdown.

Finance: The science of the management of money and other assets.

Freshman: A student in the first year of a U.S. high school or college.

Heisman Trophy: An award presented each year to the most outstanding college football player.

Interception: A pass in football which is caught by the opposition.

Junior: A student in the third year of a U.S. high school or college.

National Football League (NFL): A league of professional football teams, consisting of the American and National Football Conferences.

NCAA: An organization which oversees the administration of college athletics.

NFC: The National Football Conference. One of two conferences in the NFL.

Offense: The part of a team which controls the ball and attempts to score.

Passing Rating: A system used in the NFL to measure a quarterback's efficiency passing the football.

Professional: A person who is paid for their work.

Rushing: To move the ball by running.

Quarterback: The player on a football team who leads the offense by controlling the distribution of the ball.

Scholar-Athletes: An award given to collegians who excel in both athletics and classroom studies.

Senior: A student in the fourth year of a U.S. high school or college.

Sophomore: A student in the second year of a U.S. high school or college.

Super Bowl: The championship of the NFL, played between the American and National Conference champions.

Territorial Governor: An official appointed to govern a territory.

Touchdown: An act of carrying, receiving, or gaining possession of the ball across the opponent's goal line for a score of six points.

Varsity: The principal team representing a university, college, or high school in sports, games, or other competitions.

Veteran: A player with more than one year of professional experience.

Index